The Boy Who Made Things Up

The Boy
Who Made
Things Up

Written by
Margaret Mahy

Illustrated by
Jenny Williams

Orion
Children's Books

The Boy Who Made Things Up originally appeared in
The Chewing Gum Rescue and Other Stories
first published in Great Britain in 1982
by J.M. Dent & Sons
This abridged Early Reader edition
first published in Great Britain in 2014
by Orion Children's Books
a division of the Orion Publishing Group Ltd
Orion House
5 Upper Saint Martin's Lane
London WC2H 9EA
An Hachette UK Company

1 3 5 7 9 10 8 6 4 2

A catalogue record for this book is available from the British Library.

ISBN 978 1 4440 1131 9

Printed and bound in China

www.orionbooks.co.uk

For Andy

There was once a dad who had
a little boy.

It was a bit of a waste for this dad to have a boy, because he was much too interested in work. He worked all the week and then, at the weekends, he spent his time fixing his car.

He did not have much time
to spend with his little boy.

This was not much fun. With no dad to tell him exciting stories, the boy had to make up his own stories.

One day the dad's car broke
down a long way from home
and had to be taken to a garage.

He decided to make the best of it, and take his boy for a walk.

"Come on, Michael," he called. "We'll wander down to the cross-roads, shall we?"

Michael was delighted to go for a walk with his dad. He marched cheerfully along beside him.

After a while he said, "Shall we just walk along, Dad, or shall we make some of it up?"

"Make some of it up?" said the puzzled dad. "Oh well, whatever you like, Michael."

"Shall we go by **that** path
then?" said the little boy,
pointing. Over the field ran
a path that the dad did not
recognise. It was narrow, and a
bit tangled, with bright stones
poking through the ground.

"That's funny!" said the
dad. "I've never seen that path
before. Where does it go?"

"It goes to the sea," said
Michael, leading the way.

"But the sea is so far away,"
cried the dad. "It can't lead to
the sea."

"We're making it up,
remember," said Michael.

"The sea is on the other side
of that little hill," Michael
went on.

A soft murmuring
filled the air, as if giants
were breathing quietly
in their sleep.

The dad and Michael hurried up the little hill. There on the other side was the sea.

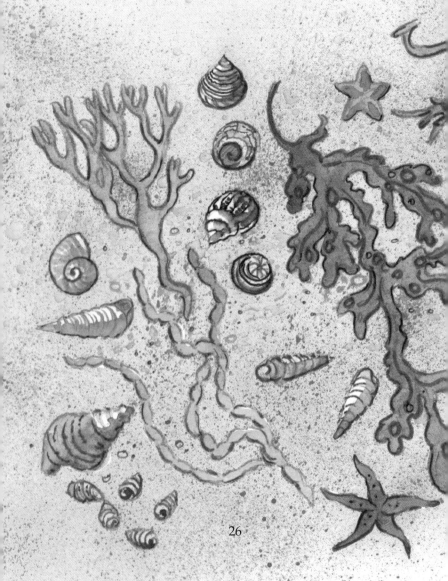

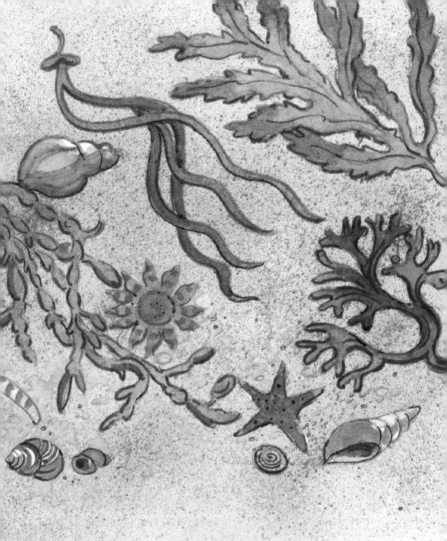

The sand stretched a long
way, starred with shells and
seaweed.

There was no one else on the
long sunny shore.

There weren't even any
seagulls – just the sand, with
the sea dancing along its edge.

"I told you. I told you,"
yelled Michael, and charged
on to the beach.

"If I'd known we were coming here," his dad said, trying hard to make his voice sound ordinary, "I'd have brought buckets and spades."

"There are buckets and spades over by that log," Michael told him. "And our swimming trunks! Mine are wrapped up in a blue towel. What about yours?"

"Er …" said his dad.

"Just make it up," Michael cried. "I'll make it up for you. A red towel, almost new."

The log lay half in, half out
of the sand, as if it was trying
to burrow down and get away
from the sun.

"Swim first!" decided Michael. "It's a bit cold. Let's make it a warm day."

Immediately the sunshine grew hotter. The dad stood frowning at his towel.

"I'm ready," Michael said,
dancing before him. "You're
slow, Dad. Last one in is
nothing but a sand-flea."
He sped, running and jumping,
into the waves.

The sand-flea dad followed.
"Be careful!" he shouted. "I
haven't done much swimming
for a few years."

"Say you're a wonderful
swimmer!" said Michael.

"Say we can both swim to
the islands."

"The islands?" said the dad.
Sure enough, out on the horizon
were islands scattered like
seeds.

The boy and his dad swam
out to the islands without
feeling tired. The water was
warm, yet tingling, and as
clear as green glass.

Bright fish, as small and
shiny as needles, followed
them and tickled their feet.
Down, down, far down under
the water, the sand shone
silver.

The boy and his dad swam
in and out among the islands.
Waves burst on the rocks
around them and rainbows
in the spray curled over their
heads.

41

Sometimes they swam
on their fronts, peering down
through the clear water,
watching fish and sand.

"I could swim all day,"
the dad cried.

"But we've got to get back
to our ice-creams," declared
Michael.

So they swam back to
the long, empty beach, still
quiet except for the sighing,
breathing sea.

"Where will we get ice-creams?" asked the dad. "There are no shops."

"Can't you understand how things work yet?" Michael cried despairingly. "We make something up! Look!"

Far down the beach something was moving closer and closer.

It was a tall thin man dressed in black and white squares. He was holding a blue frilly sunshade over his head with one hand and carrying a basket in the other.

As he passed them he put the basket into Michael's hands. Then he turned his bicycle and rode straight into the sea.

For a few minutes his blue sunshade bobbed above the water and then a green wave curled slowly over it, like a curtain coming down at a theatre.

The basket was full of
ice-cream with nuts in it, and
strawberries on top. The dad
looked very thoughtful.

After they had eaten the ice-cream, they played with their buckets and spades for a while, and then they decided it was time to go. All the way home the dad looked more and more thoughtful and grown-up. Every time he looked at Michael he blinked.

As soon as they got home, Michael was sent to wash his hands. His dad stood beside his mum, drying up the dishes she was washing.

"Tell me, my dear," he said,
in a quiet, nervous voice. "Does
Michael often make things up?"

"Oh yes!" said his mum.
"He's always making up some
adventure. He's very good at it."

"But," said the dad in a very astonished voice, "he took me to the beach. We went swimming. I got sunburned. My shoes are full of sand. And yet I know the sea is very far away."

"Oh yes," said the mum, "I told you before, but you were too busy listening to the car."

"It's very strange – very strange," said the dad.

"But lots of fun!" the mum added.

"Yes, I suppose it is," said the dad. He thought some more. "I don't think I'll spend so much time with the car from now on. A dad and son should see a lot of each other, don't you think?" he asked.

"Oh yes, I'm sure they
should," said the mum, and
she smiled a smile that was
almost a grin at the saucer she
was washing.

the orion star

What are you going to read next?

Have more adventures with
Horrid Henry,

or save the day with Anthony Ant!

Become a
superhero with Monstar,

float off to
sea with
Algy,

or have your very own Pirates' Picnic.

Grow carrots with

Lottie and Dottie,

make magic with
The Witch Dog,

and cast a spell with

The Three Little Magicians.

Enjoy all the Early Readers.